HEART

Like a Broken Arrow

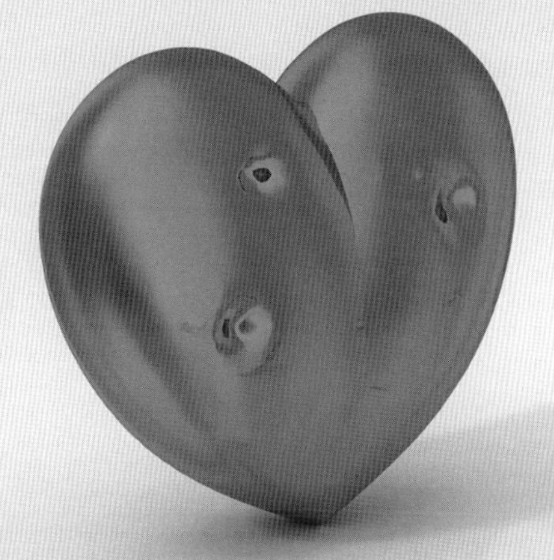

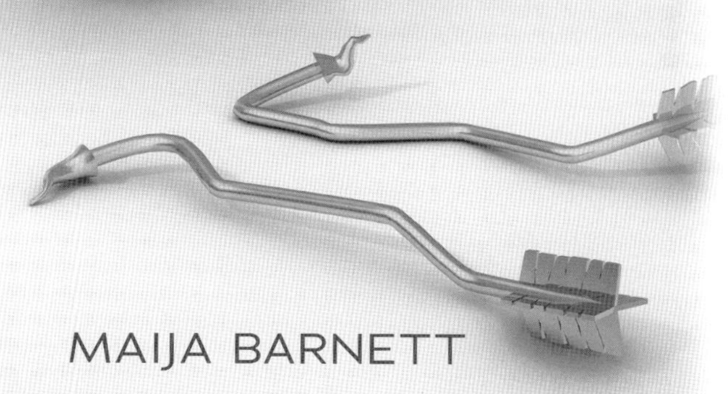

MAIJA BARNETT

An imprint of Enslow Publishing

WEST 44 BOOKS™

Please visit our website, www.west44books.com.
For a free color catalog of all our high-quality books, call toll free 1-800-398-2504.

Cataloging-in-Publication Data
Names: Barnett, Maija.
Title: Heart like a broken arrow / Maija Barnett.
Description: New York : West 44, 2023. | Series: West 44 YA verse
Identifiers: ISBN 9781978596504 (pbk.) | ISBN 9781978596498 (library bound) | ISBN 9781978596511 (ebook)
Subjects: LCSH: Children's poetry, American. | Children's poetry, English. | English poetry.
Classification: LCC PS586.3 B376 2023 | DDC 811'.60809282--dc23

First Edition

Published in 2023 by
Enslow Publishing LLC
2544 Clinton Street
Buffalo, NY 14224

Editor: Caitie McAneney
Designer: Leslie Taylor

Photo Credits: Cover and interior pages (image) Photobank.kiev.ua/ Shutterstock.com.

Printed in the United States of America

CPSIA compliance information: Batch #CW23W44: For further information contact Enslow Publishing LLC, New York, New York at 1-800-398-2504.

For Calista and Lyla

AFTER

Fast,
that's what they called me
before it happened.

Sometimes I try to forget that person.
Remembering her
makes my insides hurt.

Makes my mouth fill with the taste
of blood.

It was all so quick.
The rise of the hill.

The deer's wide eyes.
Bright in my headlights.

I can still see the snowflakes
on my truck's broken windows.

Their frozen bodies
calling me home.

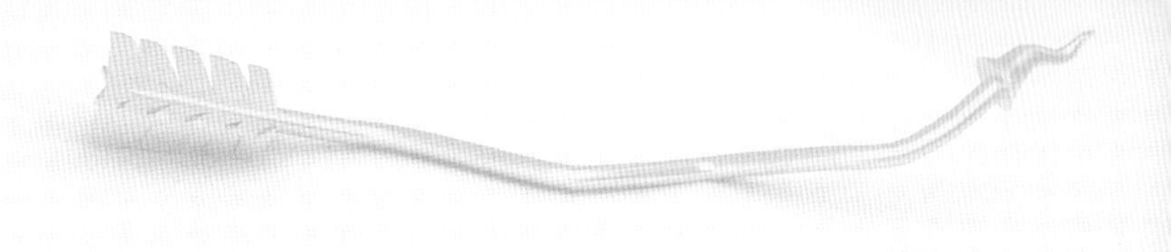

RACE DAY, AGE 17

Feet pounding.
Eyes ahead.

I know there are others behind me.
But it's like they're not there.

Instead all I see is the
October sky.

The finish line's ribbon
shivers in the wind.

Mom calls running
my ticket to college.

My feet have to take me
since money
can't.

But I don't care about that.
I just want this
thumping
in my chest.

This feel of my mind
turning off.

WHY I DON'T TALK ABOUT MY LITTLE BROTHER

I don't talk about him
because
he's gone.
And by gone I mean
not alive anymore.

Mom buried his photos deep in the attic.
Cleaned out his room.
Gave his toys away.

As if hiding that he'd ever lived
would help her somehow.
Would make it easier

for her
to forgive.

LOSING NOAH WHEN I WAS NINE

I remember the river
pulling him under.
His four-year-old voice
calling me.

"Fern!"

Mom asked why we dared
to play by the water.

I could see in her eyes
it was all
my fault.

DAD'S TRUCK

It used to be his.
But now it's mine.

(It's not like he really left it
for me.)

He just left.
And it stayed behind.

Taking up space
in our dusty driveway.

Like his words still
take up space
                in my heart.

DAD

I was 15 when he left,
but he took his time.

A little bit of him
faded
                    every day.

After Noah, he wouldn't
look me in the eyes.

Couldn't.
He said,
"It's too painful to see."

(He told me this when I was 10.)

It was my birthday,
and Mom had bought a cake.

But I couldn't choke one bite
                    down.

'Cause I knew what Dad meant.
My eyes *are* like Noah's—

pale and gray as the morning
rain.

Whenever I see them in the
bathroom mirror,

I know what it is
that made Dad
run.

DRINKING WITH JENNY...

is always fun.
Because we never get caught.

Here's what we do:
We put the good stuff in a glass.

Then we fill those pretty bottles
from the kitchen tap.

Drinking with Jenny
makes my insides smile.

Makes my mind go blank.
Just like running.

But it also makes
my heart laugh.

Jenny shouts,
"You have to work hard to play hard!"
And both of us take
another gulp.

JENNY AND ME

Jenny and me,
we go way back.

To little-kid swings.
And nap time
on the rug.

To sleepovers and movies,
popcorn in our hair.

Hers blonde and mine brown.

To sharing secrets
and laughing in the dark.

Sometimes best friends
are closer than sisters.

Even if they don't
share the same blood.

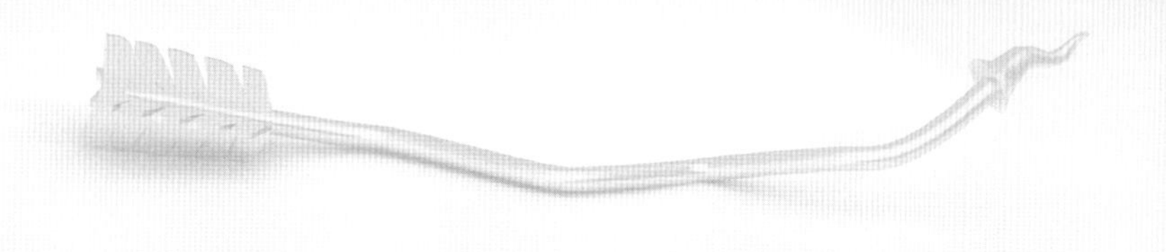

MOM'S JOB

Most days, Mom sleeps late.
She curls beneath her yellow covers.

A soft cocoon,
keeping her safe.

But on Tuesdays and Thursdays
we leave together.

We climb into her rusted Camry.
Both of us
off to school.

Mom goes to Union Elementary.
I go to Montpelier High.

On those days,
I pack
her lunch.

Even though she never thanks me.
Even though she doesn't say much
at all.

But I want her to make it
through the day.

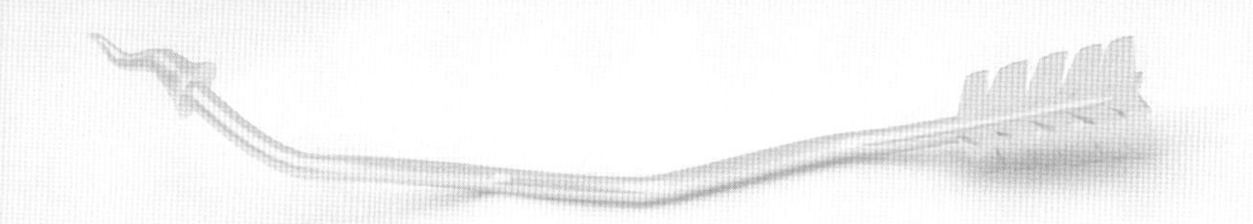

I need her to work
in her school's
busy office.

So I won't have to worry
anymore.

NIGHTMARE

In my dream we're playing
"Stamp It Till You Break It."

We're dancing at the water's
edge.

Then Noah steps onto the frozen
Winooski River.

And I hear that awful
snap.

Fear blasts through me,
trying to break free.
But I push it down and
dive in.

Ice slides past.
I dog-paddle forward.

My purple snow pants
weighing me down.

Then a flash of blue—
Noah's winter coat.

I can tell he's not too far
away.

"Noah!"
I scream for my baby brother.

I reach for him,
but the river's on me.

Its muddy water
hungry and strong.

"Noah!" I sob.
"Come back!"

I'm still calling for him
when I wake up.

JENNY SAYS

Jenny says,
"Let's have some fun tonight!"

I say yes
because I need fun.

It helps me forget about Mom
and money.

And how I don't have much of either
right now.

Jenny says,
"There's a party at Kevin's.

It's in the field
behind his house."

I squint into
the glowing sunset.
And watch pink
spread
across the sky.

Jenny says,
"Pick me up at eight!"

She flicks her hair.
It gleams like water.

I stare past her
down the thin dirt road.

My legs waiting
for a chance
to run.

LUCKY

The thing about parties is
they're not much fun.

I don't know why
I always forget.

Jenny runs off
right when we get there.

Laughing and dancing
to the pounding bass.

Someone hands me a beer.
I drink that and
another.

Then the world
softens and spins.

I know this feeling.
It's almost like running.

Like the hard parts of me are
melting
away.

"Fern, you OK?"

It's Josh from algebra.
His glasses glow
in the firelight.

I smile because
I know he likes me.
Even if he doesn't really know me
at all.

Snow starts falling.
It's getting late.

Mom warned—one more time
past curfew
and she'd take
the truck.
Sorry, Jenny, I text.
Can you find a ride home?

She texts back googly eyes,
which makes me smile.

Neither of us knows
how lucky she is.

How my single text
just saved
her life.

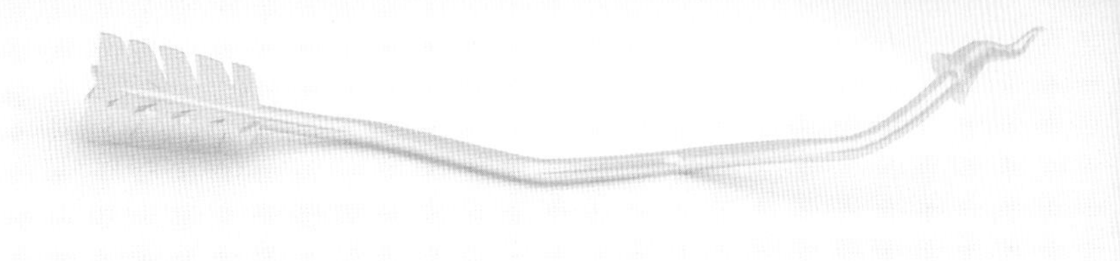

THE CRASH

It's strange,
but I don't
remember much.

Just the deer's
wide eyes.

(The November snow
made it hard
to see.)

I swerved.

Then the truck
flipped.

There was no pain.
Just my fear for the deer.

Such a beautiful creature.
I needed it
to live.

I heard screaming and thought
it was somebody else.

It wasn't until later
that I learned
it was me.

WHITE

That's all I see when I
wake up.

White walls.
White sheets.
White noise.

The buzz of the hospital's monitors.
A plastic tube
snaking
into my arm.

I know where I am
but not why I'm here.

And why am I all alone?

TRAPPED

The back brace is like a cage.

Why don't I feel like me
anymore?

The hospital hums
while I try not to cry.

My heart's beating
like I've run for miles.

I can't turn my head.
So I just stare.

Counting the tiles
on the yellow ceiling.

I reach out my hand,
but nobody's
there.

WAITING

Mom's with me now—
watching TV.

Neither of us knows what
to say.

All I know is that we're waiting.

For the doctor.
For answers.
For what to do next.

The first time I woke,
they said,
"Wiggle your toes."

I thought I'd done it.

But when I looked at the nurse,
her mouth was a
worried line.

She said, “It’s fine.
We’ll try again.”

In my mind, something wiggled.
I could feel my feet.

They were sliding over sea-green
pastures.

Cutting through cowpaths.
The wind in my hair.

But the nurse’s face said
I was wrong.

Someone should tell her
her bedside manner
sucks.

Then came the tests.
CT Scan.
MRI.

No one told us
what they saw.

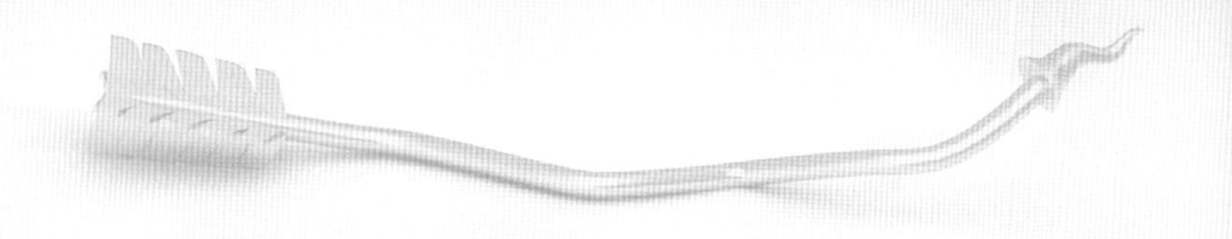

Now Mom and I wait.
Pretending we don't know the answer.

When really,
it's the questions
we need to understand.

ANSWERS

No one has to tell me.
I already know.

My bones are there.

Buried in my thighs
like hidden treasure.
Lost for good.

Mom holds my hand when they say it.

I try
not to cry.

Paraplegia—
my T10 crushed.

Someone gives me a printout
of a human spine.

My injury is circled
like a mistake.

They say I am lucky.
I can use my arms.

They say I am lucky.
I am breathing
on my own.

Lucky—
does that word
                mean anything?

Because how is any of this

lucky

at all?

WHAT I CAN'T DO

I can't go to the bathroom anymore.
I have a tube that I pretend
isn't there.

I can't leave my bed.
Or take off my brace.
Or have a shower.
Or walk.
Or run.

The nurses give sponge baths.
So I can't have privacy.

They turn me
so I won't get sores.

I can't take a walk
down a quiet street.

Legs stretching
with the rising moon.

LEAVING THE HOSPITAL AFTER TWO WEEKS

Today, I'm leaving
and going to rehab.

Where I'll learn how I'm
supposed to survive.

My arms work.
I can feel my chest.
Lungs pulling hospital air.

But below my belly button,
it's like nothing's there.

Except for my feet.
They dance and twitch.

Sending signals that never reach
my brain.

JENNY

Jenny hasn't called.
I don't know why.

Most days, Mom comes
and visits me in rehab.

But not Jenny.
She hasn't returned my texts.

Carol, my occupational therapist,
says she's seen this before.

"Sometimes," says Carol,
shaking her head,

"sometimes, darlin', it's all too much."

She tells me this while
sitting behind me.
Holding my waist
so I don't fall.

Then she asks me to reach down
and grab a ball.

It sounds easy.
But it's not.

I wobble twice.
Almost slide out of my chair.

But Carol has me.
She keeps me safe.

I wish Jenny were here.
We might even laugh.

But instead I just stretch
toward the tiled floor.

Holding my breath.
Trying not
                to cry.

WHAT I CAN FEEL

My face.
My hands.
My arms.
My chest.

My tears.

Part of my stomach.
But then things start
to fade.

If you run a finger down the arch
of my foot,

it feels like a whisper
of what I've lost.

WHEN MOM VISITS REHAB

Each time she visits,
she talks about money.

Wonders how long it will be
until I'm done.

"It's only been six weeks," I say.
"I'm not ready."

Mom says, "You better get ready, fast."

Money is short.
She hasn't heard from Dad.
Soon we'll be doing this
on our own.

THE BIGGEST CHANGE

When Noah was little,
we'd ask,
"Do you have to go potty?"

I remember Mom paying him
in M&M's.

"Just go, Noah," I'd say.
"Then we can do
something fun."

He'd climb onto
his plastic toilet.

Mom and Dad
would smile and clap.

The nurse showed me how to
insert the catheter.

How to give myself
an enema.

She clapped when I got it.
Just like Mom did for Noah.

For a moment, I wished she'd had
M&M's,
too.

THERAPY

Dr. Julie is my therapist at rehab.
She has short, gray hair.
A friendly smile.

She tries to get me to talk
about Mom and Noah.

About how it feels
to be me right now.

Sometimes, I answer her questions.

But mostly I sit.
And think about running.

The feel of the wind on my face.

Heart pounding as bold
as the bluest sky.

IF I COULD TALK TO DAD, I'D SAY...

When I was small,
you held my hand.

Checked for monsters
under my bed.

When Noah came,
you smiled at me.

But after he died,
your smile did, too.

I wish you were here
to help me through this.

To tell me
I'm still

your little girl.

ME, AFTER MISSING TWO MONTHS OF SCHOOL

Mrs. Melbourn, my tutor,
is here.

The school sends her
every week.

As if I care about
keeping up.

She drops off page after page
of Algebra II.

Some short stories for English.
A history sheet.

I shut my eyes when she asks about
last week's work.

Then wait for her to
disappear.

STANDING

Today I'm using a
standing frame.

Putting weight on my bones.
Keeping them strong.

I hold the padded handles,
and stare out the window.

It's my last day here,
and I'm afraid to go.

At home we have stairs.
There's no one to help.

I picture Noah's photos
deep in the attic.

And wonder if Mom wants to
hide me there, too.

GOING HOME

A nurse wheels me up to Mom's Camry.
The January wind cold on my face.
Then I transfer myself
into the front seat.

It's hard, but I do it by myself.

Mom stares blankly,
unsure how to help.

Someone shows her how to
fold up my wheelchair.

I try to pretend
I'm not alone.

NOT LIKE HOME

I'm sleeping downstairs on the sofa.
Mom says I'm lucky the guest bath has
a tub.

She's brought my clothes down,
in two messy suitcases.
Everything else is upstairs.

When we get home,
Mom goes to her room.
I hear the door shut.
And then, silence.

My wheelchair barely fits
through the kitchen doorway.
The living room furniture
makes it hard to get around.

The house is the same.
But I'm not.

This isn't home anymore.

MOM

Mom sleeps a lot.
Which is good, I guess.

Because she hasn't made me
go to school.

Instead I just
sit.

And watch TV.

And wish that my life would
change.

NOT GETTING AWAY WITH IT ANYMORE

Today, a social worker comes.
When he knocks on our door,
Mom tells me
to lie.

"Don't tell," says Mom,
still in her pajamas.
Rubbing the sleep
from her eyes.

"OK," I whisper.
But it doesn't matter.

He already knows I haven't been going
to school.

"But Fern doesn't want to,"
says Mom.

The social worker ignores her.

"Fern," says the social worker,
his eyes
on mine.

"You've been home
two weeks.
You're seventeen.
Don't let this
ruin your
life.

You have the weekend
to get ready.

If you're not in school
on Monday,
I'm going to
call this in."

He frowns at Mom.
And I know that I'm going.

Know there's no other
choice.

WHY I'M NEVER GOING BACK

Because it was awful.
Everyone stared.
Jenny didn't even look
my way.

I struggled with my wheelchair.
Bumped into a desk.
The halls were so crowded,
I could barely get through.

I dropped my math book and
couldn't pick it up.
Hot tears came.

I blinked them back.
But inside I was screaming.
Why does this have to be so hard!

WHAT'S NEXT?

It's been three days.
And I haven't been back.

Mom's stayed silent.
But I can feel her watching.

Trying to decide
what to do.

VISITOR

Today, Mom tells me,
Aunt Helen's coming over.

"Aunt Helen?" I say.
"Who is she?"

"She's your grandmother's sister,"
says Mom.
"On your father's side."

For a second, I see
Dad's sad eyes.

Mom touches my arm.
Then pulls away.

GREAT AUNT HELEN

Great Aunt Helen
has dark gray eyes.
Her white hair's twisted
in a bun.

She stares at me through
gold-rimmed glasses.

Says she wants me to live
with her.

"I've got space," she says.
"My husband Willard was like you.

Broke his back when his tractor
flipped."

"Besides," she says.
"You're family.
When your mom reached out,
I had to say yes."

THE TALK

"It's not like that,"
says Mom.

But she won't look at
me.

"I just can't care for you
anymore.

And with you not going
to school ...

what else can we do?"

CAR RIDE

I'm sitting
in the front seat of
Helen's van.

It has a lift.
So it was easy to
get in.

Helen smiles at me,
then turns the key.

I can feel Mom watching.
So I close my eyes

and try to pretend
I'm somewhere
else.

TALKING WITH HELEN

We're heading to Highgate.
That's Northern Vermont.

On 89, Helen
cracks open her window.
Lets the cold February air slip in.

In the sun, her white bun
glitters like snow.
But her eyes are warm,
and her voice is, too.

"Don't worry," she says.
"This is gonna be fun.
I know for a fact that
Lady will love you."

"Who's Lady?" I ask.

Helen laughs.
"Just wait and see!"

LADY

Well, now I know
who Lady is.

She greets me with her
black tail wagging.

Pink tongue
hot in my ear.

"She's not always such a lady,"
says Helen,
shooing her away.

But I already love
this sweet-faced dog.

Lady follows us
inside.

Guides me to the kitchen.
The first-floor bath.

Once I realize this house is
built for wheelchairs,
I start to
relax.

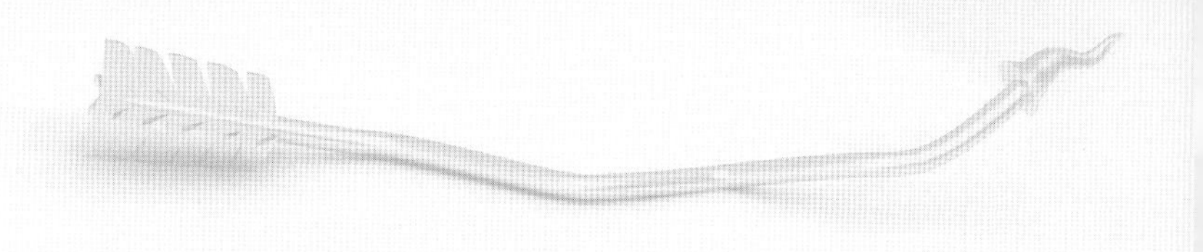

Then Helen shows me my room,
and Lady leaps
on the bed.

That's when I know
I've found
my home.

MEETING ASTRID...

The path to the barn is
perfectly paved.

It's easy to roll my wheelchair
down.

I follow Helen,
and Lady follows me.

Once we're inside, I smell
manure and hay.

Two brown eyes stare at me.

"This is Astrid," says Helen.
She gives the cow a pat.

"I think the two of you
will be fast friends."

...AND THE REST OF THE CREW

After Astrid, I meet
Silly-Billy and Buttermilk.

They're the two goats
in the next stall.

I hear chicken sounds.
And Helen calls
the Three Stooges.

Moe and Larry are the same
burnt brown.

But Curly is a speckled
black and white.

She hops in her henhouse
and coos at me.

"Curly's my best layer,"
says Helen.

"Just wait until
tomorrow morning.

I'll show you how to
collect
their eggs."

TO BE LIKE THE CHICKENS

Helen says that she has
chores to do.

She's a nurse
so she needs to make
patient calls.

She tells me she'll be on the phone
in the kitchen.
The cell service sucks,
so yell if I need anything.

I sit in the barn
and pet Astrid's black and white
side.

She leans down and rests her head
on my arm.

I watch the chickens
like they're on TV.
They hop around the coop
that's inside the barn.

Then they skip outside
and scratch dirt.

Gobbling up
what only they
can see.

I eye them through the
open doorway.
And wonder at how
peaceful they are.

Who would have thought
I'd want to be like
a chicken?

Happily pecking.

No worries
at all.

FIRST NIGHT AT HELEN'S

My first night at Helen's,
I dream about Noah.

He's pulling me down to the river's
floor.

"Stop!" I scream,
water rushing my throat.

On the shore,
Mom and Dad
turn away.

"Noah," I beg.
"Please! Let me go!"

But instead, he just drags me to
deeper water.

Until all I can see
is liquid black.

WAKING FROM MY NIGHTMARE

I must have screamed
because
Lady's beside me.

Her cold nose
pressed
to the back
of my hand.

I reach out and stroke her
silky fur.

Relieved that I'm
no longer
alone.

JUST HELEN

"Should I call you Aunt Helen?"
I ask.

"No," Helen smiles.
"Just Helen is fine."

She's fried Curly's eggs
for breakfast.

I collected them this morning.

Wheeled my chair up the
chicken coop's ramp.

It took a few tries,
but I made it to the nests.

Then I reached in and swiped
the still-warm eggs,

while the Stooges
pecked up the yard.

It felt good to do something
by myself.

Helen didn't even help.
She just told me what to do.

She watched by the barn door
as I
let myself in,

excited to do
something new.

OUR FIRST BREAKFAST

Helen talks about
Great Uncle Willard.

About how hard it was.
How he wanted to
give up.

"That tractor may have
broken his spine," says Helen,

"but I wouldn't let it
break
his spirit, too."

Her eyes grow wet.
And she grabs my hand.

"Just like I won't
for you."

SOMEONE ELSE

I used to love showers.
The water hot
on my skin.

I'd close my eyes
and disappear.

Now I sit
on a plastic chair.
The showerhead
in my hand.

I know I'm lucky the bathroom's
set up for this.
Lucky that Helen
took me in.

But as I spray
my broken body,
I still wish
this wasn't
me.

LYING IN BED, THINKING

Tonight I'm stroking
Lady's head.

And wondering why Mom
hasn't called.

It's been four days.
Is she thinking
          of me?

Or maybe she hopes
I'm gone
          for good.

TODAY IS FRIDAY

I've been at Helen's one week.

Most days I sit with Lady and Astrid.
Watching the Stooges
cluck around.

And Silly-Billy and Buttermilk eat
everything in sight.

Being here has helped me
forget about Jenny.

About how Mom hasn't called.
How I haven't heard from Dad.

But things are changing.
Helen's already warned me.

Soon I'll have to go to school.

PHONE CALL

Mom's voice cracks
when she finally calls.

She says it's the connection.
But I'm not so sure.

"Miss you, honey,"
she says.

Then we both
get quiet.

Neither of us
knows what
to say.

IT'S SATURDAY

And I'm in
the barn.

Later we're going to
physical therapy.

But this morning
is just for me.

I roll up and down
the dusty aisle.

Peek into all the
stalls.

There's one stuffed with hay
for Astrid and the goats.

One with a wheelbarrow.
A line of
old tools.

Something green peeks out
from behind
a pitchfork.

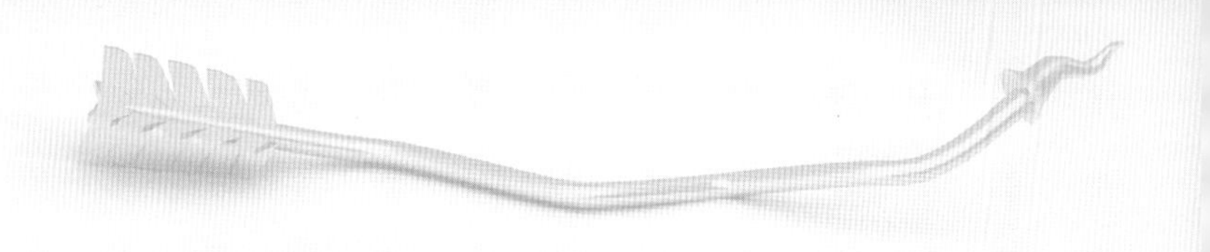

I wheel myself closer,
so I can see.

And there they are.

A set of green-winged
arrows.

Their bright feathers
calling me.

PAYING FOR PHYSICAL THERAPY

My new physical therapist
is in
Saint Albans.

It's a red-bricked town
that's smaller
than Montpelier.

Though, somehow,
it still feels
like home.

Once we're inside,
Helen
talks to the receptionist.

My heart hurts when she
writes a check.

Helen sees my face
and gives me a
smile.

"Don't worry," she says.
"It's an insurance thing.

Your mom and I will make
them pay."

HELEN'S QUESTION

At Helen's,
our milk
comes from Astrid.

In the early mornings,
Helen heads
to the barn.

A milking bucket
in her hand.

Last night she asked
if I wanted to come.

She smiled
when I told her
yes.

HOW TO MILK ASTRID

Roll your wheelchair next to Astrid.
(Helen helps me do this.)

Clean her udder
with a rag and
warm water.

Tell Astrid
she's a good girl.

Get Lady to stop
kissing your face.

(Dogs aren't allowed
to milk
cows.)

Do three squirts
to make sure the milk's good.

Then start milking.
Don't pull too hard.

Just squeeze
and release
until all the milk's
gone.

Then grab the next teat,
and do the same.

When you're done,
tell Astrid
you love her.

And give Lady a kiss
'cause you love her,
too.

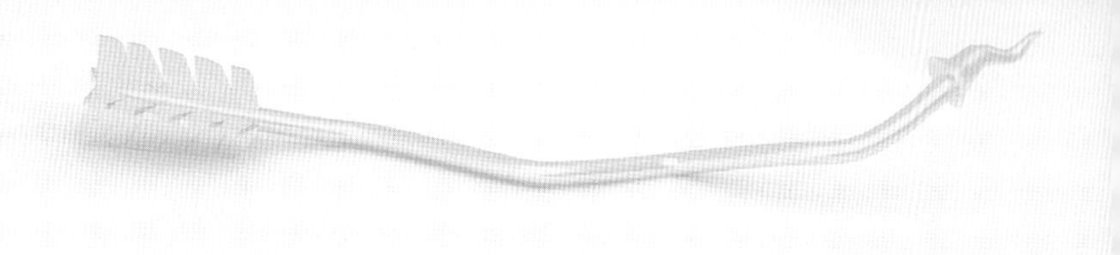

FALLING

We're in the barn, milking,
when it happens.

Astrid steps to the side,
and I lean too far forward.
Suddenly, I'm on the floor.

"Helen!" I scream.
But she's already beside me.

"I can't do this!" I say.
Tears start to come.

"You can," says Helen.

Why does she sound so certain?

"Willard did it, and so can
you."

WHY I DON'T TOUCH HELEN'S LIQUOR

It's not that I don't want to.

I'm just afraid of
what might happen.

Of what it could do
to who I am
now.

ASKING HELEN

Tonight I ask Helen
about the green-tipped arrows.

She says they were
Great Uncle Willard's.

He used them after he broke
his spine.

She tells me they used to
shoot together.

Then asks if I want to try.

Something inside me
twists
when she says that.

I think of my feet
striking pavement.

Blood rushing
through my veins.

This wouldn't be that.

But could it be something else?

Or maybe it will be nothing
at all.

TALKING TO DAD

"Dad,"
I say to the face
in the mirror.

Even though it's
only mine.

"I miss you, Dad.
I wish you'd forgive me.

I wish you could
be here
for me
now."

THE ARCHERY SET

Helen takes the bow
from its spot
in the barn.

When she hands it to me,
I hold the wood
to my cheek.

Smooth and cold,
and so much power.

The green-tipped arrows
lie in my lap

like sleeping comets
waiting to fly.

FIRST TIME SHOOTING

Helen takes me
behind the barn.

Drags out an ancient
bale of hay—
a printed target stuck to it.

She yanks the armrests
from my chair.
Gets two Velcro straps.
Slides one around my waist.
Tightens the other
over my thighs.

My feet twitch like they sometimes do.
As if they aren't mine.

"OK," says Helen.
"Now we'll shoot.
The straps make it so you can't fall."

She takes my left hand.
We pull the bowstring.
She's guiding me through
what to do.

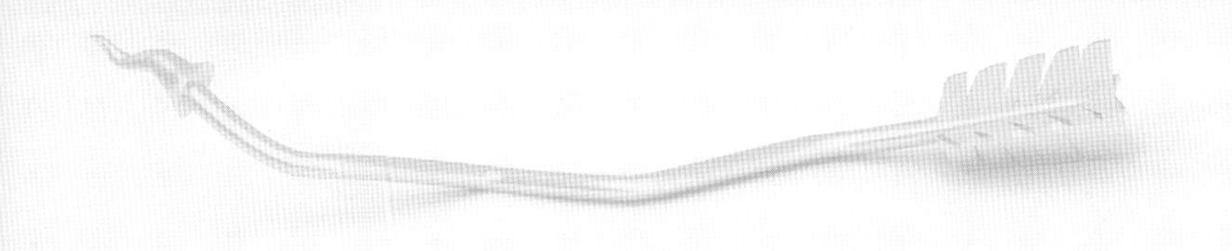

"Breathe," whispers Helen.
My arms shake.
Why does this feel so strange?
My core is numb.
So everything's off.
It's like I'm shooting with half of
myself.

"Push back in your chair," says Helen.
"It'll help with balance."

It's hard, but I try.
Working all the stomach muscles
I can.

"Now let go!" she cries.
Our arrow flies.
And something inside me does, too.

HITTING SOMETHING

All afternoon I've been hitting
nothing.

First with Helen,
then on my own.

I've practiced pushing my back
into my wheelchair.

Helen's straps
keep me safe.

My arms ache,
and my heart does,
too.

This isn't like
running.

I can't fade away.
This takes all the focus I have.

But then there's that sound.
I can barely believe it.

The heavy thwack.
I made a hit!

I wheel over to the hay bale and
blink hard.

There's my arrow,
way outside the target.

But at least I hit the hay bale.
That's all I need.

HELEN TALKS ABOUT MY DAD

His mother, Jessica, was my
older sister.

Just 16 months—
so not much older at all.

As kids, we didn't get along.
I thought she was silly.
She thought I was a pain.

We drew a chalk line
down the center of our room.

Neither of us
dared to cross.

When we grew up,
we grew even further
apart.

I hardly saw your dad
when he was young.

Willard and I
couldn't have children.
So we weren't invited to
children's things.

Maybe Jessica was afraid
she'd hurt our feelings.

Or maybe that chalk line
was still drawn
in her heart.

If there's one thing I regret,
it's letting that happen.

Letting my sister and her family
drift away.

"WHAT HAPPENED TO JESSICA?"

"She died," said Helen.
"Before I could fix things.

Before I knew
I had something
to say."

PRACTICE

Thwack.

That's the sound of me
hitting the target.

Every day I come out here and shoot.

It's been almost a month.
And it's hours of effort.
Helen thinks I'm obsessed.

But I'm an athlete at heart.

And shooting helps me forget
what's changed.

When my mind is centered
and my aim is true.

It's like I become someone else.

THE DREAM

Tonight I dreamt
that I was running.

I ran past the farmhouse,
Lady at my side.

Dust rose behind us.
It must have been summer.

The garden was
a rainbow
of light.

Helen was there,
smiling and waving.

While my feet pressed on
toward the bluest
sky.

MOM'S CALL

"Fern,"
says Mom.

"I just talked to
Helen.

She says
you're going back
to school."

My stomach drops.

But I knew
this was coming.

Inside, I want to
run.

NEW HIGH SCHOOL

Missisquoi High.
That's where I'll be going.
Helen set up a tour.

When I think about it,
I want to hide.

Because I don't see how
I can be that girl.

The one who's trapped in
the metal wheelchair.

The one who's so different
from everyone
else.

SHOPPING

Today we drive to Burlington
to get new clothes before my tour.

In the mall, I can feel
everyone staring.

I want to leave,
but Helen says no.

"You're going to school," she says.
"You have to get used to things."

"Please," I whisper.
"I'm not ready for this."

"Then get ready," says Helen.
And for the first time since I've met her,
she sounds exactly like my mom.

THINKING ABOUT HELEN

Sometimes I wish
she was
my mother.

I've only known her for a month.
But I like the way she smiles at me.

Makes sure I've eaten.
Takes me shopping—
even though it was hard.

Checks in before bed.

Those are things
a mother does.

But not my mother.
She locks herself
in her room.
And doesn't speak to me
at all.

MY PHYSICAL THERAPIST

My physical therapist's name is
Misty.
She's young and pretty
with white-blonde hair.

She can't believe how well I'm doing.
How strong my arms are.
My balancing skills.

When I tell her about archery,
she thinks it's great.

She says she'd love to see me shoot.

"Have you thought about joining
a club?"
she asks.

I swallow hard and say,
"Not yet."

ONE GIRL SHORT

This morning we tour
Missisquoi High.

Helen comes, and I'm glad.
I can't face this on my own.

The building looks like
my old high school.
Same classrooms, library,
and lockers, too.

There's an elevator, which is good.
But the hallways feel narrow
in my chair.

They have a student lead us around.

Her name is Mia,
and she's tall and thin.
Red hair in a messy bun.

During the tour, Mia talks to Helen.
It's like
I'm not there.

I know why that is.
I know what she sees.
A metal chair.
Not a girl, like her.

"Fern likes archery," says Helen,
when we're almost done.
"Mia, the office staff said
you do, too."

Mia turns and stares.
She's taking me in.
Like she finally sees me.

"I'm on a team," says Mia.
Her voice is small.

"Right now, we're
one girl short."

TOMORROW IS MONDAY

I wish I could stay in the barn
forever.

Listen to the Stooges
peck and cluck.

Feed Silly-Billy and Buttermilk.
Kiss Lady's wet nose.

But tomorrow is Monday,
and that means
school.

Somewhere I'm afraid
to go.

Helen said Mia,
our red-haired tour guide,
will meet me
at the door.

I guess she's in a bunch
of my classes.

So she offered to help me
get around.

That should make me feel
better,
but it doesn't.

I don't need anyone's
pity.

And I don't want to think about
all those
eyes.

SUPPER

"First-day jitters?"
asks Helen,
passing me the rice.

"I wonder if we'll hear from
your mom?"

But we don't hear.
The phone stays silent.

And I don't get
a single
text.

I go to bed
with an ache
in my chest.

Wishing Monday would never
come.

LISTENING

I'm lying in bed, waiting for sleep,
when I hear Helen on the phone.

"Nathan," she says.
"Don't do this.

She's your daughter.
She needs you."

Is this a dream?
No, I'm awake.

I feel Lady's nose pressing
into my arm.

As if she knows
my father's voice.

As if she can tell
I'm afraid.

FIRST DAY

Helen touches my cheek
when she drops me off.
"Be brave," she whispers.

I want to cry.

But instead, I wheel myself down
the concrete walkway.

Cool March air on my skin.

Eyes searching for
red-haired Mia.

Heart hoping I'll make a friend.

MIA BROWN

Mia meets me in the lobby.
Says she's sorry about before.

"I was nervous," she says.
"I didn't know what to expect."

I carefully look her in the eyes.
"I'm just like everyone else," I say.

"I know," says Mia.
"Can we start again?"

"OK." I try to smile.
Then, we head to class.

Later, Mia invites me to sit with her
at lunch.

Her friends are there,
but they act like I'm normal.

Though I can feel them watching
when they think I'm not.

No one asks me
what happened.
They're too polite.

When archery comes up,
Mia looks at me.

"Can you stay after?" she asks.
"My dad teaches PE.
We can use the school's archery set."

"Sure," I say.
Mia smiles.

That's when I think I've made a
mistake.

Shooting is something I do on my own.

How do I know
I'm ready to share?

SHOOTING WITH MIA

I see some kids on the bleachers.

I can tell they're not watching—
just joking around.

I miss my straps.
But at least my armrests are off.

I sit in my chair, hands sweating.
Mia sets the target up.

Then the world narrows.
I take a shot.

In my mind, I can feel the arrow hit.
I've gone somewhere else
when I hear Mia say,

"Wow, Fern!
You're not bad!"

MIA'S QUESTION

"Join our team,"
says Mia.

"We need a third.

Ask your aunt about
Catamount Peak Archery.

We could really use you."

IN THE VAN

"How was your day?"
asks Helen.

"It looks like you
made a friend."

"I think I might have," I say.
"She wants me to join
an archery club."

"You mean Catamount Peak?
You know, Willard shot there.

That sounds like the perfect
plan."

UNSURE

I'm in bed.

Lady's on the floor
beside me,

her head resting
on my arm.

I finished my homework,
which wasn't so bad.

The only thing tripping me up
is math.

I guess I didn't see my tutor
enough.

I guess I didn't really
try.

But that's not why I don't know
what to do.

I'm not sure I should join
Catamount Peak.

I haven't been shooting that long.
And it won't be like running.

I can't hide
in my head,
eyes set on the
distant sky.

This will be different.
There'll be more
talking.

I'll have to deal
with everyone
else.

FIRST FRIDAY AFTER SCHOOL

Well, I made it through Friday.
That's a relief.

My mind aches from schoolwork,
but I wasn't alone.
I ate with Mia
every day.

Found out she has a younger brother.
That her mom's a teller
at a bank.

I know she volunteers
at an old-age home.
That she wants to be a nurse.

All that time, I learned about her.
I didn't say much
about me.

WHAT MIA DOESN'T KNOW

She doesn't know
about my little brother.

That my best friend still won't
talk to me.

That drinking made me
crash my truck.

That I haven't seen my dad
in years.

All she knows is that
I like archery.

And that she wants me
on her
team.

SATURDAY MORNING IN THE BARN

"Do it," says Helen
once the milking's done.
"You need this.
It'll be good for you."

"But I've only been shooting a month,"
I say.
"I'm not even
very good."

"You practice all the time," says Helen.
"I have to drag you in at night.

And besides, who cares how good
you are?

There's more to life than being
the best."

STARTING AT CATAMOUNT PEAK

Helen drops me off at
Catamount Peak.

There's an outdoor range
where everyone's standing.
Even though it's late March.

It's work pushing my wheelchair
over the field.
But I told Helen I didn't need
help.

I'm just thankful that
there's not much snow.

Once I get there,
an instructor walks over to me.
He's wearing a camo vest.
His gray hair is
military short.

"I'm Todd Campbell," he says.
"You Fern?"

I nod.

“Nice to meet you,” he says.
He holds out his hand like I’m
anyone else.

“You might be wondering why we’re
outside,” says Todd.

I shrug and try to smile.

“Team likes it more.
So I let them choose.

Now I’m looking forward
to seeing you shoot!”

THE TEAM

Mia shows up before we start.

She gives me a hug.
Says she's sorry she's late.

Then she introduces me to everyone.

Lily is short with curly brown hair.
A perfectly made-up face.
She says hello
without a smile.

Barry and Martin are brothers.
They look about 12.

They wave and continue
goofing around.

Then a boy steps up from behind
and my breath almost stops.

"This is Jay Runner," says Mia.
She grabs his arm.

He grins and gives her braid a tug.

"Hi," I whisper,
my mouth going dry.

Jay is stocky with
dark hair and eyes.

When he smiles,
I want to
disappear.

"Our team's small," squeals Mia,
as Jay lifts her into the air.

"But all of us are
pretty good."

"Oh," I say,
my nerves kicking in.

When Jay smiles at me,
my heart beats fast.

And I feel like I did
when I used to
run.

SHOOTING

We take turns shooting.
Three arrows at a time.
I strap in and pull my armrests off.

My first two shots miss the
target completely.
Stick angrily into the ground.

Stop it, I think.
Forget where you are.

I pretend I can't feel the others staring.
I hear someone say,
"How's this gonna work?"

I close my eyes and remember running.

When I look up, it's like
the target's inside me.

I aim, take a breath, and release.

PERFECT SHOT

"Well," shouts Todd.
"I think we have our third member.
That is, if you'll have us," he says.

I smile and nod.
Mia grabs my hand.

Lily nods but doesn't smile.

From the way she shot,
I can tell she's the best.

Jay cocks his head
and stares at me.

His deep-set eyes,
taking me
                in.

THE NEW ME AT SCHOOL

No one knows me as the girl
who wins every race.
The girl with the truck,
whose dad ran off.

The girl with the chance
at a scholarship
they secretly think
she doesn't deserve.

Instead, I'm the new girl.
I'm Mia's friend.
The girl in the wheelchair
whose secrets are safe—

locked inside
her pounding heart.

PRACTICE

Practice is
Tuesdays, Thursdays, and Saturdays.
We shoot outdoors.

When I'm there,
I try not to think about Jay.

My arrows become part of me.
I see the target
in my mind
and start to hit it
more and more.

I forget about those
deep-set eyes.
The sound of his voice,
joking
with Mia.

The feeling he sees my chair,
not me.

MISSING JENNY

I wish Jenny were here.

I could tell her
what it's like.

To like a boy,
but be trapped in a
wheelchair.

To feel like running
to him.

But be unable
to stand.

To wonder if he'll ever

really see
me.

FIRST COMPETITION IN BENNINGTON, VERMONT

"It's six rounds.
Four shots each," says Todd.

The warm April wind
ruffles my hair.

Mia and Lily
smile and nod.

Inside, my heart
is a frightened
bird.

MY SHOTS

Something happens
when I shoot.

I go
somewhere else.

I know Helen's watching.
And Jay is, too.

But I don't think about them.

I just
strap myself in.

Let my mind
become the arrows.

Nothing else
matters
at all.

THIRD

Mia's beside me
leaping up and down.
She reminds me a little of Lady
right now.

Jay's staring like he actually
sees me.
Not my wheelchair.
Not what I can't do.

"We came in third!" squeals Mia.
"Out of 20 teams!
Lily was second, I was fourth, and you
were tenth!

I'm so glad you joined our team,"
she says.

Inside my heart,
I can run.

MIA AND JAY

"We've been best friends
since we were small,"
says Mia.

We're sitting outside
during lunch.

It's late April now.
All the snow is gone.
(Not that we had much
anyway.)

I tilt my face
toward the sun,

letting its heat
soak my skin.

"We've never dated,"
says Mia.

"I don't see him
that way.

Anyway, I just thought
you should know."

Mia tosses her hair.
It glows
like fire.

Inside my chest,
my heart
grins.

AFTER PRACTICE

"Fern,"
says Jay,

while I'm heading to
             Helen's van.

"Do you think you'd want
to go out
sometime?

I stop and stare.
Am I hearing him right?

"Me and you?"
             I say.

"You and me," says Jay.

He smiles.
And I smile back.
"Sure," I say.
Is this a dream?

"How about this Saturday
after practice?"
he asks.

His dark hair gleams
in the fading light.

"After practice,"
I say.

Then Helen waves.

"See you Saturday," he says,
as I roll away.

Behind me I hear
Mia whoop.

"See?" she screams.
"I told you she'd say yes!"

WHAT I'M AFRAID OF

I'm afraid of what it means
to like somebody.

To have this body
with the things it can't do.

"Oh, Lady," I whisper
in her fuzzy, black ear.

"I almost wish
I'd told him
no."

MY DATE WITH JAY

Jay comes in his truck
to pick me up
for our date.

Then he asks if I mind if he
picks me up, too.

"OK," I say.
He slips his arms
around me.

My heart skips when he rests me
on the passenger's seat.

Then he folds up my wheelchair
and sticks it in the back.

Climbs in and says,

"You ready to go?"

IN THE TRUCK

Jay's voice is soft
when he talks about himself.

How his dad works for Vermont's
border patrol.

How he's part Abanaki
on his father's side.

How he doesn't like
going to school.

What he does like is archery
and four-wheeling in the woods.

The feel of the earth beneath
his tires.

Racing through the trees.

BEST DATE EVER!

At first, I'm scared.
I've never done this before.

Even when
I could walk.

But Jay helps me up
and settles me behind him.
Tells me to hold tight
to his waist.

And then we're four-wheeling.
The sun in our eyes.
The wind
streaming
through our hair.

I press my cheek into
Jay's back.

Heart pounding at the thrill.

ALMOST LIKE RUNNING

"What'd you think?" asks Jay,
grinning at me.

We've stopped in a
sunny field.

Dandelions dot the grass like treasure.
Jay's eyes shine in the light.

"It almost feels like running,"
I say.

He touches my hair
and kisses me.

Then he smiles and revs
the four-wheeler's engine.

We laugh beneath the early May
sky.

LEARNING MORE ABOUT JAY

Helen walks over when Jay
drops me off.

"Jay Runner," she says.
"It's so nice to see you.

I bet Astrid would love it
if you stopped by."

"You know Astrid?" I ask.

"Jay helped when she
went lame," says Helen.
"He used to shadow one of the
local vets."

"I'd love to," says Jay.
We head to the barn.

Lady trots at my side.

IN THE BARN

Jay rubs Astrid
behind the ears.
She nuzzles him,
eyes closed.

"I didn't know you want to be a vet,"
I say.

"I don't," says Jay.
"I just tried it out.
That's why I shadowed Dr. Black.

But after we put down
my neighbor's horse ...

well, that's when I knew
it wasn't
for me."

LUNCH WITH MIA

"I'm so glad you and Jay
are dating," says Mia.

She takes a gulp of
cafeteria milk.

"Dating?" I say.
"We went out once."

"But you like him?"
she asks.

I feel myself
blush.

Mia laughs.
"Well, he told me
he likes you,
too."

TELLING MOM

Today when Mom calls,
I tell her about Jay.

Right after I've said it,
I know
I've made
a mistake.

"A boyfriend?" says Mom.
Her voice is a
blade.

"How is that even possible
for someone
like you?"

CRYING WITH HELEN

Helen finds me sobbing
into my pillow.

Lady's beside me,
starting to howl.

"Oh, sweetie," she whispers
when she hears what Mom said.

"Don't listen to that.
It's not true.

Willard and I stayed married
after what happened.

We loved each other.
So we made it work."

HELEN'S EYES GROW WET

She runs her hand down
my spine,
stopping where
I can no longer feel.

"Jay likes you
for who you are," she says.

"Everything else is
nothing at all."

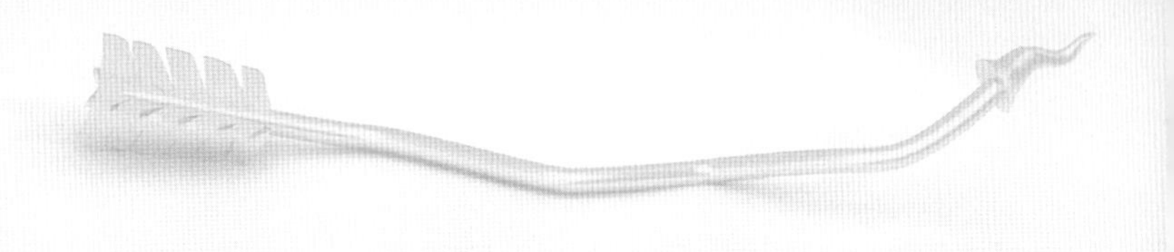

BEING WITH JAY…

makes me forget
who I am.
What I've lost.

All I feel are his lips on mine.

My arms, around his waist.
As we four-wheel through fields
dotted with flowers.

Laugh in the library,
studying for a test.

Or sit in the barn
stroking Astrid's sweet face.

It's only been a month.
But I feel like he knows me.

Better than anyone has before.

SITTING IN JAY'S TRUCK

His hand in mine.
My head on his chest.

It's Saturday evening and we've been
four-wheeling through the woods.
Racing down old snowmobile trails.

The windows are open.
I hear the spring peepers
singing to me in the coming dark.

Then Jay whispers something in
my ear.
His words are so soft,
I almost don't hear.

"I think I love you," says Jay.
He squeezes my hand.

I squeeze his hand back and say,
"Me too."

MIA'S 9:00 P.M. CALL, TWO DAYS LATER

"He's leaving," sobs Mia.
Her voice fades out.

"Mia" I say.
"Are you still there?"

I press the phone to my ear
and roll into the kitchen.

The spot near the stove
is usually good.

"Who's leaving?" I ask.
But my heart
knows.

"Jay," she snorts.
I start to go
numb.

"His dad's getting sent
to the Texas border.

They just found out today.

They're packing the house
and moving next week."

I want to comfort my friend.
But I don't know
how.

Instead I just peer out
the kitchen
window.

Watch the moon rise
behind the barn.

SAYING GOODBYE

"Mia told you," says Jay
after knocking on my door.

It's 10:00 p.m.
And he didn't ask to come over.

He just showed up,
eyes red from tears.

"Yeah," I whisper.

"I told her not to," he says.
"I wanted to tell you on my own."

Jay touches my hair
while I try not to cry.

Then he lets his hand
drop to his side.

"I'm sorry,"
he whispers into the darkness.

"I never meant to do this.
But we'll be so far apart.

I won't stop you from meeting
someone new."

"But what about what you said
in your truck?" I ask.
"Was any of that even true?"

My face grows hot.
"It was," says Jay.

*I feel like something inside me
is breaking.*

"Fern," Jay whispers.
He leans down and kisses my cheek.

Then, before I know it,
he's gone.

THE SAME OLD FERN

It's practice today.
Only, I'm not going.

I don't want to be there.
My heart just can't.

For a moment, I was happy.
I was making it work.

This life without parents.
Without being able to walk.

I was becoming
someone new.

But now all I am is
the same old Fern.

The girl who's not worth
anything at all.

LUNCH WITH MIA

"You broke up?" gasps Mia.
I try not to cry.

"Oh, Fern, I'm so sorry."
She grabs my hand.

Mia's eyes are puffy.
Her beautiful hair is in knots.

"I can't stand that he's moving,"
she whispers to me.

"We've been neighbors forever.
Now there will be some stranger
next door."

I close my eyes and try to imagine
Texas.

But I can't make myself
see anything at all.

NOW THAT JAY'S GONE

I can't think during practice.

I picture his face
and miss every shot.

Now that Jay's gone,
I dream about Noah.

I see his small body sinking
to the river's bottom.

My throat raw
from screaming his name.

Now that Jay's gone,
I can't do my homework.

I just sit in my wheelchair,
Lady at my side.
And wish this were happening
to somebody
else.

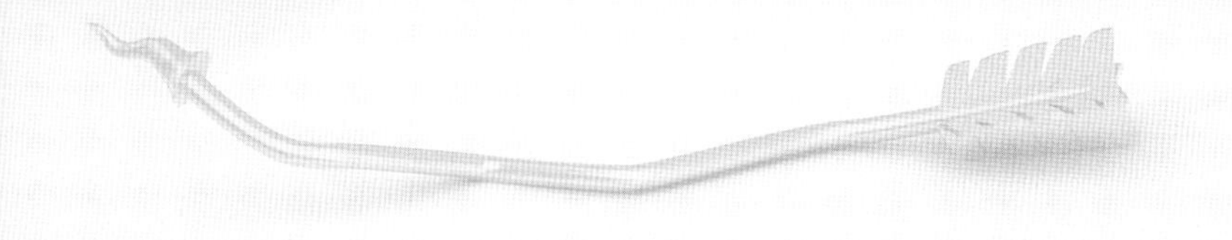

DRINKING AGAIN

Tonight,
Helen is working late.

I milk Astrid.
Feed the Stooges and the goats.

Then Lady and I
slip into the kitchen.

I open the cabinet beneath the sink.
Searching for what I know
is there.

The golden scotch
tastes like poison.

But once it hits my brain,
I no longer
care.

SAVED

"Fern!"
Cold water splashes
my face.

"Oh my god, Fern.
Please, wake up!"

I open my eyes,
and Helen's above me.
Eyes wild, face white.

"Oh, thank goodness," she cries.

Then she presses me
to her.

Her tears hot
against
my skin.

WHAT HELEN DOES

"This can't happen again,"
says Helen.
Her hand is on mine.

"I need to be able to trust you."

"You can."
My voice shakes when I say it.

She frowns and starts
opening cabinets.

Pulling out bottles of
liquid gold.

"You don't have to do that," I say.
Helen shakes her head.

Then dumps each one
in the kitchen sink.

CHOICES

Helen and I sit at the
kitchen table.

She tells me choices
must be made.

"You can't go on like this," she says.
"I saw it happen to Willard.

When the darkness comes,
you need to find the light.

Before Jay left,
you were doing fine.

I know it's only been two weeks, but
it's time to start accepting things."

"I know a way," I whisper.

"I know you do," Helen says.
"Now you just have to
make it work."

"Are you going to tell Mom?" I ask.

Helen frowns.
Runs a hand
though her snow-white hair.

"Let's see what you choose,
OK?

Then I'll decide
what I'm going
to do."

HOW HELEN HELPS

She takes a leave from work,
so I'm never alone.

After dinner and milking, we
practice archery.

She's a good shot,
but I've grown better.

She cheers every time I get a
bullseye.

Tells me I'm going to kill
at States.

She checks on me each night.
Kisses my forehead.

Says I'm the daughter
she never had.

NEW THERAPIST

My new therapist's name is
Lucy Higgins.

Her purple office
smells like lilacs.

Her smile is kind.
And she nods when I talk.

"You've been through a lot," she says.
I blink back tears.

"But I'm glad you feel comfortable
coming here."

Then Titan, her cat,
leaps onto my lap.

Rubs his face against mine and
starts to purr.

WHAT TODD SAYS

After practice today, Todd pulls me aside.

"Something's changed," he says.
His eyes are wide.

"You've been struggling
the last couple weeks.

And now, suddenly,
you're not.

I've never seen you
shoot like this.

It's like something inside you clicked.

I think you have a chance to be
top in the state."

The others are listening.
I see Lily's face.
Curly hair pulled in a
ponytail.

Perfect makeup—
so her acne's almost
not there.

I know she dislikes suddenly
not being the best.

But I can't help myself.
I have to
try.

MIA AND ME

Mia grabs my arm after Todd
walks away.

"You heard that?" I ask.

"Everyone heard,"
she grins.

"Before we had you,
we didn't have enough girls
for a team.

Now that you're here,
we might actually win!"

She throws her head back,
and the sun catches her hair.

It glitters like a
queen's crown.

This is the first time I've seen Mia smile
since Jay moved away.

My heart hurts
when I think about him.

Mia sees it in my face
and gives me a hug.
"We don't need him to be happy,"
she says.

Then why do her eyes look
so sad?

"Besides, without Jay, the boys don't
have a team.

But you and Lily and me—
we're gonna win!"

MESSAGE FROM JAY

When the message pops up,
my heart drops.

I don't want to read it.
What if he found
someone new?

Don't be stupid, I think,
rolling into my bedroom.

From my window, I watch Astrid chew
the spring grass.

Clovers dot the glowing green.

Just get it over with! I think.
Then I open the message.

It's just a photo of
Jay's face.
Same dark eyes.
But his hair's gotten longer.

Hope you're OK!
it says.

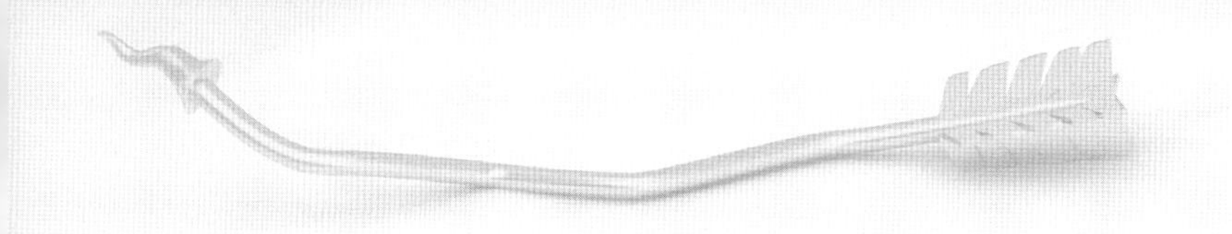

The tears start to come.
Why do I miss him
like this?
We dated less than a minute.

So why does it hurt?

My therapist thinks it's not about
who he is.

It's what he means to me.

"And what's that?" I asked her.
Wanting to know.

"Acceptance," she said, smiling wide.

"The knowledge that someone can
love you
for you."

THESE DAYS

These days I
study hard.

These days my mind clicks.
And my body does, too.

In English, we're reading
The Odyssey.

I think I'm like Odysseus
with his bow.

The one that only he
could draw.

The one that saved him
in the end.

But my enemies aren't
evil suitors.
They're my own fears.
My own self-doubt.

I think of him when I
aim at a target.
When I study for a test.

And I try not to wonder about
my parents.

About how Mom and I haven't spoken
in over a month.

Instead, Helen and I talk
about college.

How it's possible again.

With me shooting so well,
I could get a scholarship.

Maybe my life is about to
begin.

JUNE SLEEPOVER

Mia sleeps over two weeks before States.

We visit Astrid.
Feed the Stooges and the goats.

"You have so many chores," says Mia.

"I love it," I say,
remembering how hard it was in
the beginning.
"It proves I can do anything."

"Fern," says Mia, looking away.
"Why do your feet twitch sometimes?"

My face grows warm.
But I'm glad she asked.
"It's because my nerves can't talk to my
brain," I say.

"Oh," says Mia, looking sad.
"I hoped it meant you might
walk again."

TELLING MIA

It's midnight when I tell Mia
what happened.

To Noah.
To Mom and Dad.
To me.

But at least now she finally
knows me.
Now she understands
who I am.

When I'm done, she stays quiet.
"Mia?" I whisper.
Scared she's like Jenny
after all.

"You're a brave person," says Mia,
grabbing my hand.

"And I'm really glad we're friends."

TALKING WITH MOM

"Fern?" It's Mom.

I'm in the kitchen.
Helen has just passed me
the phone.

"Helen said you made the
state archery tournament.
She asked me if I want
to come."

My hands shake when I think of
seeing my mother.

Of having her
watch me shoot.

"OK," I say.
My voice is a whisper.
Part of me wants to tell her
no.

THE NIGHT BEFORE STATES

The night before States,
I dream about Noah.

We're back at the river
holding hands.

I'm nine.
And I'm in my
purple snow pants.

Tears are running
down my cheeks.

"Don't cry," says Noah.
He smiles at me.
"You know it's time for me to go."

"Don't leave," I beg.
"You don't have to!"

But he's already stepped onto
the frozen Winooski.

With my next breath,
he's gone.

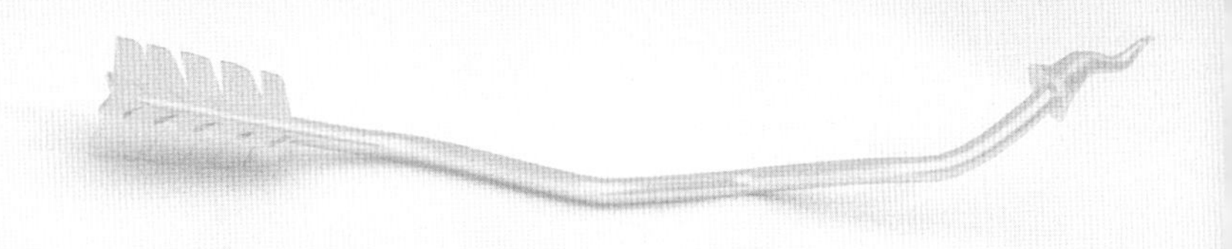

“Noah!” I call to the
empty river.

“Stay brave,” says a voice,
in my ear.

“Noah?”
My eyes search
the water.

But all I see is ice
and snow.

LEAVING FOR STATES

We milk Astrid
in the dark.

The late spring moon
glows white.

Then we lock Lady
in the house.

She barks and howls,
but we can't take her.

Though I sure could use her love
right now.

As I sit, silently in the car,
scared of what's
coming next.

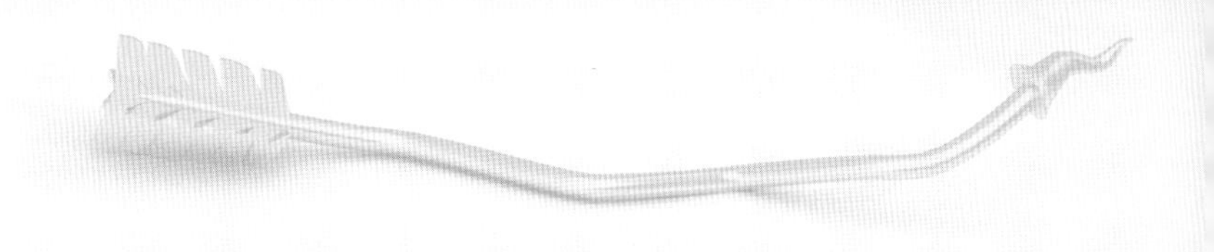

THERE

Todd meets us at the indoor range
in Saint Albans.

It's 6:45 a.m., but he wanted us early.
That way we could get a feel
for the place.

I've competed before.
But not like this.
I'm glad I listened to Todd's advice.

I find Mia and Lily
waiting outside.
Both of them holding bows.

Their families are with them.
Todd waves them away.

But not before Lily's dad yells,
"Go get 'em, champ."
He says it to Lily,
but his eyes are on me.
Baseball cap turned
to the side.

Then Lily takes his hand
and leads him over.

"Dad," she says.
"Here's the girl with the real chance
of being
            champion."

"You must be Fern," he grins.
I start to relax.

Then he looks from his daughter
to Mia
            to me.

"You three are gonna strike 'em dead!"

"Dad!" says Lily.
And that's when I finally like her.

Because I know she sees us
as a team.

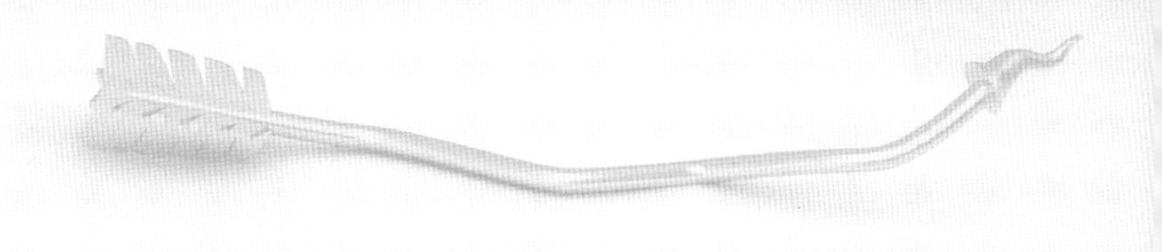

HELEN

"Be brave," says Helen.
She kisses my cheek.

"And don't think about what's
happening around you.

Just focus on what
you came here
to do."

She squeezes my hand,
then heads to the bleachers.

White hair disappearing
in the crowd.

SHOOTING INDOORS

I've never shot indoors before.
Since I joined the team
late in the year,

all our competitions have been outside.

It's loud and bright.
Just like the school gym.

The crowd sits on bleachers
behind us.

The targets are down the far end
of the room.

When we first walk in,
I see the press
setting up.
A blonde woman leans down beside me.
A microphone in her hand.

"You're Fern Blakely, right?"
I nod.

"What's it like being the only
disabled archer here?"

A girl behind me laughs.
"We know who's getting all the press."

Lily turns and hisses,
"Shut it!"

The reporter says,
"Jed, did you get that on tape?"

I suddenly think I'm going to
be sick.

"Come on," says Todd.
"Follow me.
Fern, we need to talk."

TODD'S TALK

"As you can see, there's press."
Todd rubs his nose.
I've never seen him nervous
before.

"Just forget them.
Think about what we came here to do."

"OK," I whisper.
But I'm scared.

What if they write about what happened
to Noah?
Or even what really happened to me?

I stare at my legs.
Hating the worry
burning inside me
like a flame.

SEEING DAD

We're shooting 20 ends.
Three arrows each.
Targets are set
18 meters away.

Before shooting, I check the stands
and spot him.
For a moment, I almost forget I can't
run.

I haven't seen my father in almost
two years.

My mind goes blank.
My heart pounds in my ears.

I keep thinking of all the ways
he showed he didn't
love me.

The angry glances.
Not saying goodbye.

"Fern," Mia hisses
from somewhere on my right.

"Get it together. You have to shoot!"

I close my eyes
and think of Noah.

Hear the voice
from my dream.

"Stay brave," whispered Noah.

I love you, I think.
And I take my first
shot.

SHOOTING

My first shot misses.
But the rest
hit their mark.

Over and over,
I become the arrow.

I don't remember much.
Just the sound of my heartbeat.

The stillness I felt
when I could
run.

My feet pounding over
pavement.

Taking me where
I had to
go.

AFTERWARD

Afterward there's screaming.
Mia yells, "We won!"

She's jumping up and down
like Lady again.

But I don't care.

I just stare into the crowd,
searching for my parents.
Waiting for them.

Helen runs up.
Tears in her eyes.

She hugs me and tells me
she loves me.
Then whispers Mom and Dad
had to go.

"You mean they left?" I cry.
"They didn't want to talk?"

Anger rises inside me.
But I swallow hard.
Try and blink my tears
away.

"Your dad ..." says Helen.
"It was all too much.

He couldn't face you.
Couldn't face what he did.

Your mom is driving him
home."

"Home?" I whisper.
"You mean my old house ... together?"

"Yes," says Helen, touching my cheek.
"Maybe there's hope for them
yet."

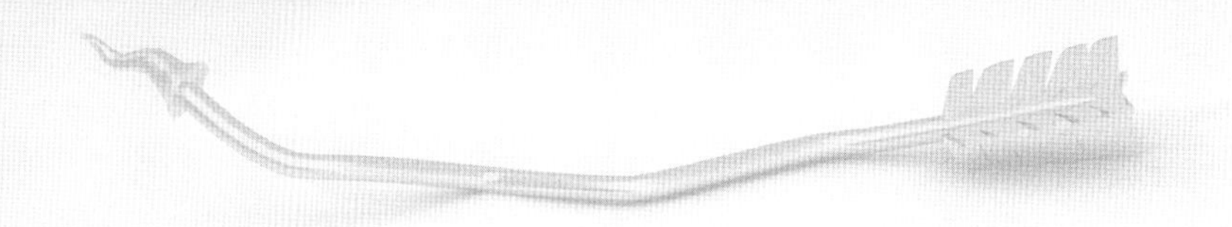

LATER

After all the pictures
had been taken.

After I'd held the team's first place trophy.
My silver medal
around my neck.

After I'd talked to the reporters
about how far I'd come.
How I'd shot second best
                in Vermont.

After the college scout told me that
Columbia would be calling.

(Helen actually clapped when she heard
that. But I just smiled and shook
                his hand.)

Later, when I sat in the barn
                beside Astrid.

Kissed Lady's cold, wet nose.

That's when I knew
where I was going.

That I'd finally found
my way.

PHONE CALL

I'm getting ready for bed
when the phone rings.

"It's your father," says Helen.
"You should take this."

I transfer myself from my bed
to my wheelchair.

Then roll into the kitchen,
heart pounding hard.

"Hello?" I whisper.
The line cracks.

"Fern, it's Dad."
For a moment, there's silence.

"Oh baby, I'm sorry I didn't stay.
When I saw you today,
I felt so proud."

"Then why did you leave?" I ask.
"Why didn't you want to talk to me?"

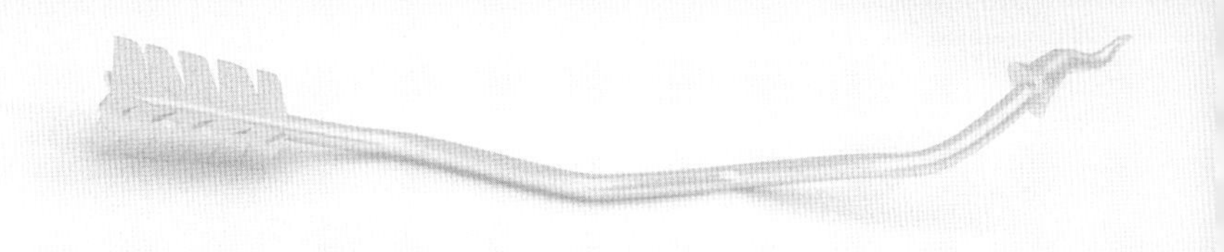

"I'm sorry, Fern."
He's crying now.
"I've been like a child.
Blaming you.
All these years, I let you suffer.

But you were a kid
when Noah died.
You were only nine years
old.

It was our fault.
We let you play near the river.

You and Noah.
We failed you both."

I don't know what to do.
He finally did it.
He said what I wanted to hear.

"Fern, it's Mom."
Dad's voice disappears.

"Your dad and I love you.
We want you to know."

"I love you, too," I whisper.
Then I hang up.

"Fern?" says Helen, grabbing my arm.
"They're trying now.
You can't ask for more.

Just remember, whatever they say,
you don't need them to forgive
yourself."

LAST DREAM

In my dream, Noah's 12.
The age he would be
if he were still alive.

I'm the age I am
now.

We're running through a
golden field.

Lady's at our heels,
jumping as we run.

Barking the way
she always does.

Noah grabs me.
We giggle,
then fall to the grass.

Our faces turn to the summer sun.

FINAL SHOT

I smile at the target,
steady my arm.
Behind me, a robin sings.

Lady's barking in the house.
Astrid's eating grass nearby.

Right now, my mind's blank.
I'm not thinking about Mom, or Dad,
or Jenny.
I'm not thinking about Jay.
Or what I've lost.

Instead all I feel is
the warm sun.
The strength of the bow.
This arrow in my hand.

I take the shot.
It's a bull's-eye.
Inside my chest,
            my heart sings.

MY HEART IS AN ARROW

My heart is an arrow,
easily snapped.

But its core isn't made from
metal or wood.

It's muscle and flesh.
When it breaks,
I bleed.

Yet I gain the strength
to heal what's lost.

So I can shoot straight
and find
my way.

WANT TO KEEP READING?

If you liked this book, check out another book from West 44 Books:

EVERYTHING YOU LEFT ME
BY PAIGE CLASSEY

ISBN: 9781978596474

INTRUDERS

Two uniforms knock
on our front door.

Panic flutters
in the pit
of my stomach.

My mother and I swap a look.
Neither finds an answer.

I CRACK THE DOOR

I've never seen the tall one before.
But the other one is
Dougie Porter.
He looks like a kid playing dress-up.

The tall one says,
"Good morning, ma'am."
His gut spills over
his belt.
A flaky breakfast crumb
clings to his collar.

"Mornin',"
my mother answers.
I hadn't heard her slip
behind me.

"Is this the Morris residence?"
he asks.

My mother
turns to Dougie instead.
"Dougie Porter,
I've known you since you were
in diapers.
You know this is my house."

Dougie scratches his neck.
Mumbles, "Yes, Mrs. Morris.
We just have to do everything by the book,
see."
His eyes sink to the ground.

Was I speeding
on my way home yesterday?
Is this about the graffiti
behind the Dollar-Rama?
Do they think I had something to do
with that?

MIXED UP

Or is Mom
mixed up in drugs
again
and hiding it well?

No More

Officer Crumb Cake
starts again.
"Ma'am, I understand you already know my partner."
He pauses
to smirk
at Dougie.

"I'm Officer McFarland.
We're looking for an
Edward Leroy Morris.
This house is listed as his last known address."

Everything stills.
Even the birds stop cawing.

My mother's voice is
quiet.
Cold.
She replies,
"Edward Leroy Morris don't live here
no more."

WHAT KIND OF CRIME

Mom starts to shut the door.

"Do you know his current whereabouts?"

She laughs.
But there is nothing
funny
or warm in it.

"Dougie, what's this about?"
I ask quietly.
He finally looks me in the face.

"Maybeth, we're looking to question him
about his possible involvement
in a crime."

I swallow.
"What kind of crime?"

"I can't tell you that. I'm sorry."

CHILL

Crumb Cake jumps in again.
Thinks he'll have more luck
with me.

"Missy, can you tell me the last time
you saw your daddy?"

I chill my voice
until it's as cool
as my mother's.

"I haven't seen my daddy
since I was eight years old.
That's going on ten years, now.
And it's Maybeth, sir.
Not Missy."

I let the door swing shut in his face.

THE
BEST
PART IS
AT THE
END

THE
DRAGONS
CLUB
CYN BERMUDEZ

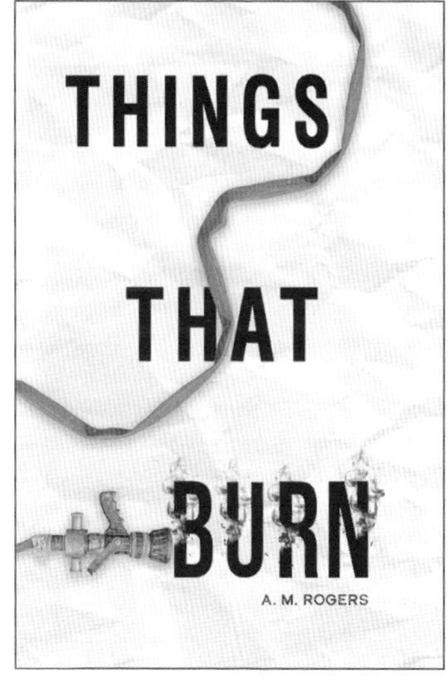
THINGS
THAT
BURN
A. M. ROGERS

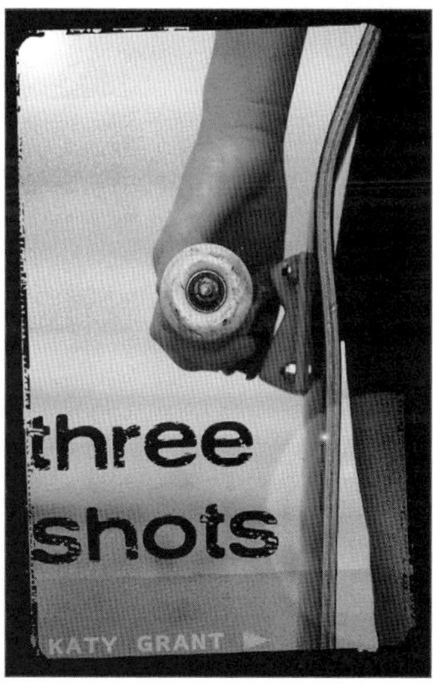
three
shots
KATY GRANT

ABOUT THE AUTHOR

Maija Barnett grew up in Central Vermont and now lives in Massachusetts with her husband and two teenage daughters. She loves nature, poetry, hiking in the woods with her dog, and finding ways to get kids excited about reading. Maija holds degrees in English and teaching and currently teaches at a school for students with learning differences.